the case of

THE
THINKING
MAN'S
TRUMPET

a Detectors mystery

the case of

THE
THINKING
MAN'S
TRUMPET

a Detectors mystery

by

PAUL MACAULEY

illustrated by

PHOEBE MUNSON

Pea Squared

ISBN: 978-1-5262-0736-4

The Case of the Thinking Man's Trumpet: A Detectors Mystery

© 2018 Paul Macauley
First published in Great Britain 2018
by Pea Squared
92 Old Shoreham Road, Brighton, BN3 6AD

Illustrations by Phoebe Munson

REGARDING THIS

This novel pertains to the precise set of circumstances and happenings that surrounded the build up to, and then actually, the theft of one of the most powerful Musical Mind Control devices the world has ever known, and the subsequent hunt for, and Detection of, such a thing by our most renownedest of Detectors and features, though is in no way limited to, and may or may not even make reference to, a chase through setting low fat margarine, a jazz bar interlude, a scrap with a bear who isn't a bear but who for the sake of this story arguably is, and the return of possibly the most devious villain in the UK's home counties/south-east region.

As with the retelling of many true stories certain narrative licenses have been taken. These include #45821: License to wield Outlandish Terms; #65421: License for the use of Unlikely Nouns and a special license granted for the creation of a custom font (upon reviewing this account the publisher agreed that a normal typeface wasn't strong enough to convey the level of drama the story climbs to. Castings were taken of a standard font and moulds created to cast new words in titanium, the only material capable of containing such lively truths).

Some names have also been changed. Bumble appears here with its silent '7' omitted and the tale's telling is littered with references to meals and snacks that were likely eaten at different times to those stated, if at all. Other than that, and even including *some* of that, everything in this novel of Bumble & Nitsy's 6th major adventure remains absolutely and wonderfully true.

You may think 'novel' is too grand a term for such a slim sheaf of thoughts. Indeed, this book may appear to be less a Jacobian banquet and more of a sweaty school trip ham salad sandwich complete with pond scum-esque wilted lettuce. Rest assured that neither is the case. Instead prepare to enjoy a sustaining narrative broth, one that will trickle past your empathy gullet and warm the very tummy of your need for solidarity in the human experience.

N. von Nitzenjammer
Brackham-on-the-Bit
December 2010

PIECES

1

BUMBLE & NITSY: DETECTORS

Bumble and Nitsy were the grandest Detectors who ever did just that. They detectored many things about the world, often without even meaning to. They even detectored in their sleep, that's how good they were. Here are some of the things they detectored in just one day: broccoli: birds-eye trees, the Mindbrella, the Goddess of Communications (Telephanie), The Tongue: Hammock of Lies, the Midnight Wizard Quilt, and the enquiries: When does a pile become a mound? How come fairies are so good at electrical lighting? Why do ovens of all appliances need gloves?

It is curious to think that even now some people don't know what detectoring is and will often put it into the same bag as detective work. This really is quite wrong.

Detective work is the vocation of the dogged and grizzled, who follow little clues, which lead to other clues, which lead to a whole nest of clues, which the detective will scoop up into a case, hence the detective procedural being referred to as such. They use this harvest of cluelets to paint a big picture in support of solving a crime.

Detectoring is by far the subtler art. Where a detective may be foxed in the pursuit of an elusive clue, a Detector would not have the same problem because they simply don't think in the same way. Detectors deal in mystery, curiosity and wonder.

An example then. Imagine the scene of what is undoubtedly a murder. A woman lies on the floor, quite, quite dead, barely a mousepace from a bloodied knife. A detective enters. They map the room, look for signs of breaking and entering. They examine the body of the unidentified woman, picturing the struggle that lead her to fall in such a way. They dust the room for fingerprints, take blood samples from the knife and courier them to a lab. Perhaps they wave one of those ultraviolet lights around. They leave, their head a tombola of facts. Frantically they dip into this clue raffle, hoping against hope they will clutch the magic number that will lead them to the murderous criminal who remains at large and still criminalating people. Weeks pass and they finally match powder blue corduroy fibres extracted from the dark blue carpet and figure that they're after somebody who wears powder blue corduroy. So the detective checks with local clothiers to enquire whether they stock such an item and if anyone has recently bought some and if so did they pay by a traceable credit card? Maybe they get an address and they raid the address and find, against all hope, and expectation that their painstaking work should pay dividends by now, that the corduroy trouser wearer skipped town weeks ago. The detective returns to the evidence room as stumped as a felled Californian redwood.

Now if a Detector were to enter that same crime scene the whole scenario would play out very differently. They might catch their pocket on the door handle and swing into the hat stand and become entangled in a scarf that smelled like a nauseating afternoon in a chemist. They would perhaps get no more than a glance at the bloodied knife before remembering that they were out of jam at home.

Detectors working as part of a team bounce into each others thoughts as a matter of course. It's likely then that the Detector's partner would understand that, yes, they may need jam, but the lack of Robblesums's Blueberry conserve isn't the major problem of the moment. The major problem of the moment is they have also run out of toilet paper. Pressed by a police chief into supplying something so limiting as a verbal supposition about the attack on the dead woman, the Detector would most likely think about going by the corner shop on the way home to pick up some bits.

In the swirl of growing voices and frustration the Detector might consider the supermarket a better option, simply because they resent paying local shop prices for premium toilet roll. Pinned against the wall by the helplessly out-of-his-depth Police Chief, with one's fellow Detector trying to strike the awful man with some wax fruit, the Detector would experience that most wonderful rush of insight that is their stock in trade. Most people experience this rarely, if ever, and label it an epiphany.

The epiphany that Bumble shouted forth into the room that day was that the murdered woman was none other than celebrated farmacist Penelope Loveslice. That she had unwittingly let her murderer into her house. That this was no random killing, but a robbery of the set of keys normally pressed into the base of the wax guava that lived in the fruit bowl on the dresser. That the police would never catch the man who did this because it wasn't a man who committed the crime, it was a mouse. A mouse who wore blue corduroy. A mouse who probably liked jam. Maybe.

The experienced Detector would be no stranger to the quiet laughter of others, even a police forensic squad. They would take comfort in the sage nodding of their partner Nitsy's head, despite him clutching a melted guava. They would follow their detectoring with a clear instruction for the authorities to search the only place such a mouse would celebrate his evil ways: the village fete. Oh, he may not be wearing any recently bought second hand doll sized corduroy, and he may or may not be eating all the jam, but by heavens he will be the only mouse in that field who smells of Ms Loveslice's perfume.

* * *

Detectors of Bumble and Nitsy's quality rarely wait around to be proven right or wrong, they soon move on to detectoring the way a cloud looks a bit like Gibraltar, or what Chinese food might be called in China. Still, when the news later came in that the killer mouse had been apprehended, Bumble and Nitsy allowed themselves a small moment of joy. They had some crumble. The mouse had been traced from the annual Brackham-on-the-Bit Summer Fete to the late Ms Loveslice's small business the Erstwhile & Somewhen Farmacopeoia. There he was arrested and charged, not only for Ms Loveslice's murder but for a string of brass faster thefts up and down the country. Everyone agreed it was a ruddy good thing Bumble and Nitsy had found the rotter.

Detectoring isn't a skill one can switch on and off at will. Even some experienced Detectors go doolally because they can't stop their minds from detectoring things. As Bumble lay on her pillow waiting for sleeptime, she couldn't help but think of Penelope Loveslice's unlikely assassin. What had his plan been if he had got into the farmacopeoia? He didn't seem the type to think too far ahead. Then, for the second time in as many days, Bumble's mind rumbled with the arrival of a train of detectorings. Of course he wasn't a mouse at all, at least not originally. And of course he hadn't been working alone; he'd been working for someone else. But who? Only one person could have reason to want to gain access to the Estwhile & Somewhen Farmacopeoia. Only one person had the power to turn a man into a mouse. It was someone

Bumble and Nitsy had met before, their most powerful and cunning adversary. Someone whom they had defeated by the narrowest of narrow whiskers and who had been banished for all time to Nothing. Or so they thought. Could this mouse have been in the employ of He Who Shall No Longer Be Cc'd?

Bumble tried to put all this out of her mind. She did not sleep very well that night (Nitsy did. He was snoring up a storm).

2

THE THINKING MAN'S TRUMPET

It had been a year since Bumble's inspired detectoring had solved the murder case of Penelope Loveslice. There had been interviews, three documentaries and invitations to speak at public events. Minor detectorings followed too as Nitsy detectored a revolutionary element for a new washing machine and managed to sell the idea for an immaculately tidy sum. Soon enough though, interest in the famed Detectors began to dwindle. They were never able to repeat their foray into crime solving and almost overnight they were taken off the police chief's speed dial. To the public, detective work and detectoring were still as different as vanilla and strawberry in a tub of Neapolitan, and the people had decided they much preferred the taste of vanilla.

With detectoring no longer paying the rent the Detectors had to return full time to their day jobs. Nitsy worked in a wall factory, while Bumble wrote for the Brackham-on-the-Bit Daily Tribune. Not always the most scrumptious ways to earn a living, but Nitsy was good at walls and people liked to read Bumble's column. The two would often meet after a day's wall making and word smithery at their favourite coffee house and tea room, *Much Ado About Muffins*. The staff there were friendly and would let the pair linger over their usual order of Milky Steam and a Hot Bean Juice.

Here is a fact about Bumble: Bumble rarely wore horizontal stripes. She feared they would make her look either a) short, b) like a bee or c) like a short bee.

Here is a fact about Nitsy: Nitsy was afraid of Sundays. One day he'd accidentally got trapped in one; the whole day had flapped up and grabbed hold of him, sticking like clingfilm that's pounced onto one's leg. He was utterly and hopelessly trapped. Bumble had been on hand to extract him and thankfully the ordeal had lasted only 24 hours.

Bumble and Nitsy's great power lay not in their skills of detectoring, unquestionable as those were, but in that they faced the days together. This was also a necessity as they often couldn't remember simple things, like their house number. They each took responsibility to remember one digit. At least three evenings out of every seven they would get to number 36 first time. And in any case they were now on good terms with the family at number 63.

On this particular day, a Saturday, Bumble and Nitsy were sat on the comfy pink sofas at *Much Ado About Muffins*, staring into space. Quite an expected pastime for a couple of Detectors you might think, and you would be right except this air gazing was down to terminal boredom. Nothing quite thrilled them as much as detectoring, but they'd accepted their days of success in that regard were long over. Icing that gloomy cake was the frownable irritation that Bumble couldn't even complete the Tribune crossword. She hot-desked in the same office at the Tribune with the chap who wrote them and it didn't seem as fun when you knew the answers. Nitsy was trying his hand at knitting a jumper, which was now twenty feet long. As fruitless as it all seemed Nitsy kept knitting his endless jumper and Bumble kept knitting her lessened brow because there was nothing better to do.

Bumble decided to reread the supplements, this time from front to back just in case she'd missed anything of interest. She was wise to do so, because she had. On page 42 of Weekend Style began a four page article on the Head of Telepathic Broadcast of Notional Instances at revered detectoring college the Thought Kitchen. Professor Darius Candlewick had begun his tenure at the Kitchen (that's what the students called it) several years after Bumble and Nitsy had completed their detectoring studies. As Bumble read on she felt it was a shame she never got to learn from the man. His dashing moustache aside, Candlewick had been quite brilliant in advancing ideas in the realm of Thought Projection, though much to the disapproval of the establishment. It seems push had arrived at shove when the professor was shown to have used college money to develop a prototype device based on his theories. His fall from grace hadn't seemed very dramatic because precious few followed the key names in theoretical detectoring. And because he was a drunk and did a lot of work to discredit himself by spending any time he wasn't lecturing in the Frick & Nesthead pub. The college had allowed that Candlewick leave with his invention and his dignity. He forgot the latter though as before he left he did a drippy-wet-wet in his trousers following a lunchtime of drinking pints of, aptly, bitter. For years his invention had remained untested and unseen by the world. Until now.

Of course, the article was a plug for something. In one week's time Professor Darius Candlewick would appear at the Natural Mystery Museum to unveil to the world, and show in action, the device that had caused him to be doused in scorn. The museum would then display the invention for only fourteen days before Candlewick again hid it away forever.

The article had a glorious two-page colour illustration of the Thought Projection instrument. Its intricate pipe work, three button controls and the brass broadcasting 'cone' had put some people in mind of a trumpet. All of this was protected by a special, advanced carry case, finished in purple suede. If you were a Detector then catching a peep at what had been dubbed by some as The Thinking Man's Trumpet was the hottest ticket in town.

"Hey, listen to this," said Bumble.

Nitsy was reading the paper. He'd given up knitting for today. The jumper was now 23 feet long.

Bumble read from the article, excited. "It works like an electrical music machine such as a Pineapple iHum, if an iHum delivered music straight into your brain without need for earphones. But instead of delivering 'Lovelysexymagic' by Justine McTimblebaum, it transmits the pure thoughts within the trumpet blower's mind."

"That's shocking," Nitsy mumbled without looking up.

"I know. The transmission of thoughts is Professor Candlewick's lifelong passion..."

"Unbelievable," Nitsy shook his head.

"...an unappreciated field of discovery..."

"That is actually criminal."

"...which the professor hopes to shed a light on at his Natural Mystery Museum demonstration this weekend."

"Why would you kill somebody for a trumpet?" Nitsy asked. Bumble frowned, she'd said no such thing. Before she could launch into her tirade about how Nitsy never listened to her, he showed her the newspaper he had been reading. The article was:

'Professor Killed In Trumpet Theft'

Professor Darius Candlewick, inventor of the Thinking Man's Trumpet, had been found dead on the steps of the Natural Mystery Museum. His great invention was nowhere to be found, presumed stolen. Bumble whipped out her Pineapple 6 and called their old acquaintance the Police Chief. He confirmed all the media had to say on the matter. But when Bumble offered the services of two experienced Detectors, he cut her short. Incredibly the police already had the name of the suspect and were minutes away from making an arrest. Bumble protested that she and Knitsy could still be of use in interviewing the suspect, but the fuzz wouldn't hear of it. He was at least good enough to tell Bumble who it was the police were after. She shivered.

Nitsy knew something was wrong when Bumble ended the call (even further wrong than a murder and the theft of a telepathic trumpet). The partners were used to the muddling of the two different flavours of detectoring and detective work; the line between the two could get distinctly mushy, especially when things heated up. Occasionally though they would be reminded that there was a third skill, a rich chocolaty stripe of evil. That there were those who would use their abilities for underhanded purposes.

Despite the urgency, Bumble and Nitsy finished their beverages (it seemed silly to waste them, even though it meant Nitsy burned his top lip), tidied up the papers (this was just good coffee house etiquette. Except Bumble took the magazine in case they got caught waiting for a train or something), had a wee (because they didn't know when they would next be near a toilet) and rushed to the scene of the crime.

The person the police were about to apprehend was none other than Phantom Pebblefoot.

3

PHANTOM PEBBLEFOOT

What could make Nitsy burn his lip with a Colombian blend? What could make Bumble's spine shiver like a noodle in the breeze? It was the thought of their arched enemy, Phantom Pebblefoot. Several words on this name would be a good thing right now, just to let you know what Bumble and Nitsy were dealing with.

The Phantom was all razorblade shadows and swift dreadspills. He lived only ever in the moonlit night-times. A person could tell that the Phantom was close when the soles of their feet began to hurt. It was a pain that jumped up and bit you like you'd got a pebble in your shoe. From then on you knew something bad was going to happen and that the Phantom would soon appear in his contorted form, leaning over to the left because his heart was full of evil (that's why he was arched. Evil is very heavy).

You see, that's the difference between the noble Detector and the shady breed that is the like of the Phantom. A Detector takes from the world little observations and details and make of them something more. It's what they learn from good (if slightly strange and drunken) mentors like Professor Candlewick (dead). Then there are deadly Detectors who are taught the craft of Projection.

What is Projection? A brief illustrative example for you: while walking on the beach, a Detector detectors that some small brown pebbles look like laminated chocolate buttons. Lovely. But a Projector is taught to detector something and twist it into its worst possible state. They amplify the negative until it rattles like weed killer through their veins. It's a frightening way to see the world. But that is not all the Projector does. They earn their name by taking that most horriblest of things and firing it into the unsuspecting mind of their victim. If all of a sudden you're beset by the stride-stopping pain of what is, in your mind's eye, the most jagged of pebbles caught in your shoe, but upon inspection you find nothing then you my friend may have been on the sharp end of a Projection.

Of all those who ever Projected, it was a boy named Philbert Drak who was the first and best in this cruel craft. As a child he would spend his days sitting in the street, waiting. When a neighbour left her house, Drak would watch her walk to the end of the road and then hurl into her mind the thought that she'd left the iron on. It made him laugh to see how she slowed down as she questioned whether or not she was worrying over nothing. If she continued on he would Project further. His victim's poor mind would be pummelled with images of melting carpets setting fire to curtains, enveloping the house in flame and boiling the fish tank. She would run back into their house and quickly realise that of course she hadn't left the iron on. She would emerge flustered, and late for the appointment she was trying to keep, hurrying unwittingly past little Philbert Drak, who was now rolling on the ground with laughter.

To his credit Drak was also a good talent scout. He could spot a fellow Projector from 3 miles away and through heavily papered walls. He also knew who he could turn to Projection by projecting into their minds the assertion that being evil would be a good career move and would get them lots of money and kisses. That's how he'd recruited Phantom Pebblefoot, so named for his expertise at Projecting into the minds of his prey the very real experience of having a pebble in one's shoe.

For a time it seemed that Drak's rise was inevitable and many feared that he would rear an army of Projectors with unstoppable power. In the end his plans were thwatered (that is to say drowned in the waters of a superbly thought out plan) and Philbert Drak was prosecuted for tax evasion. Cocky about his ultimate victory, he was nevertheless banished from all known reality and sent to

Nothing - a place that can't even be spoken of as a place because it is Nothing. At that point even Drak's name ceased to exist. For as long as his memory was in the fading thoughts of those who'd encountered him, he was occasionally spoken of as He Who Shall No Longer Be CC'd. Eventually even this slipped out of All knowledge.

* * *

It seemed that the Phantom had used his pebble projection trick to slip past security at the Natural Mystery Museum. The security guard had apparently been busy shaking out his sock, leaving his video monitors unscrutinised, allowing the Phantom to creep into the room where Professor Candlewick was setting up for the next day's Trumpet recital.

By the time Bumble and Nitsy got to the museum Professor Candlewick's well-dressed cadaver had already been removed, leaving only a small cherub of a constable named Petitfilous on guard in the old exhibition room.

"Nothing to see here," he gurbled unconvincingly. He had obviously been briefed to keep the Detectors out of the loop. Bumble sized up the lamb. She guessed he was green enough not to know that whatever he did Bumble and Nitsy were already inside the loop.

"We *are* the loop, dagnammit!" confirmed Nitsy, putting Bumble's thought into the realm of the spoken.

The constable was taken aback. Bumble shook her head. She wished Nitsy would tread a little softer sometimes. She gently rounded on the nervous young man.

"We're just here to help," she said. Nitsy peeled off and conducted a sweep of the room. He did this by rolling on the floor like he was in a barrel going over Niagara Falls. It felt more fun that way.

"I'm not going to tell you the suspected location of the suspect," constable Petitfilous puffed out his chest.

"I suspected as much," Bumble replied. Behind her Nitsy was building up quite the momentum, making the same sound as a soul singer going over cobbles on rollerblades.

"Thankfully there's not a whole lot you can tell me that's of importance," Bumble added. Petitfilous looked stung.

"Well try asking me where the Phantom is hiding," he blurted.

Nitsy was now caked in dust and fluff.

"I think I would rather ask some more relevant questions," said Bumble smoothly. Constable Petitfilous was clearly lost. "Such as why would Phantom Pebblefoot, one of the most famous Projectors in the world, steal a thought projection device that offers no greater power than he possesses already?" Bumble had him trumped.

Nitsy was mid roll when he started to gag on a large piece of lint.

"Are you saying that the Phantom didn't kill Professor Candlewick in the exhibition room with the malice after all?" asked Petitfilous. Nitsy lolled on the floor with his tongue stuck out, trying to cough out the lint. He rolled over and accidentally licked the floor. Something became stuck to his tongue. He stood up.

"I'm just saying, constable..." Bumble checked the policemen's badge, "...Petitfilous, that megavillains such as the Phantom don't pop up in the public eye for an obvious murder and a thief unless it's absolutely their intention to do so. There's something bigger going on here."

Nitsy coughed dryly.

"So you don't want to know where the Phantom is?" asked the confused constable.

"Let me guess, they've traced him to an underground lair near Cheddar Gorge?"

Constable Petitfilous nodded.

Bumble sighed. She snatched the piece of paper from Nitsy's tongue. He finished his choking, relieved. "That's exactly what he wants them to think, but they won't find him there," said Bumble, examining the slip of printed paper. She motioned to Nitsy to stop picking lint from his mouth and to follow.

"Where are you going then?" asked Petitfilous, suddenly looking very lost.

Bumble waved the paper. "To where Darius Candlewick spent the last night of his life," she smiled knowingly. She turned and walked into the door frame. She clutched her nose as Nitsy guided her out, spitting fluff.

Just like that constable Petitfilous was alone again guarding his crime scene. It had been a strange few hours. His superiors had looked very concerned at the mere mention of the name of Phantom Pebblefoot, some chap who'd apparently turned to the Drak side. Then there was this dead man who had invented some kind of trumpet, something important enough to be killed for, except the two strangers who'd just left said it wasn't and there was something else going on. It all seemed very complicated and strange and Petitfilous found himself wishing that he was back on the beat again, shovelling roustabouts off the high street outside Yates' on a Friday night. He decided he might as well focus on the positive though and pondered on the slip of paper the Detectors had found on the floor of the room. On it was written:

'You're looking absolutely lovely today'

That made him feel a little better.

4

THE NEUROTIC DANCER

It was raining when Nitsy and Bumble arrived in the filthy back alley in the middle of town. Bumble had already pulled on her squirrel hat; Nitsy was scrambling in his pockets for his own headwear, donning a hat shaped like a giant peanut. Suitable though the weather was given the moody turn their location had taken, Bumble found it very trying.

"How long is this frickin' rain going to last?" she grumbled.

Nitsy adjusted his peanut. "Until the early evening or so, then a milder front is going to start moving in from the west."

Bumble stared at him.

"So I heard," he said. "What is it we're looking for?" He quickly changed the subject. Bumble didn't reply, she just kicked her way through the soggy boxes and bags of rubbish, pausing only to tap the wall and move on.

Nitsy accepted that Bumble would answer when she felt like it. He scratched his peanut. At that moment one of Bumble's taps returned an answer and a small section of the brick wall sprung out: a doorway.

"Oooo, a hidden stripblub," said Nitsy. Bumble dragged him inside a dimly lit room, grateful to get out of the rain.

Music played from somewhere inside the building as they made their way to a small booth. The lady in the booth watched as a squirrel and a peanut hovered towards her in the dull light.

"Can you tell us if Darius Candlewick visited you last night?" Bumble enquired, removing her dank squirrel.

"Who?" asked the lady, her voice squeezed through the little microphone and speaker set into her perspex box.

"Professor Candlewick. Tall, glasses," Bumble explained impatiently.

"He had tall glasses?"

Bumble huffed.

"Perhaps one of your dancers would remember him?" Nitsy ventured.

"Maybe," agreed the lady in an unconvincing sort of way.

Bumble led them away and on into the club.

"Whoa!" squeaked the lady in the booth, "you haven't paid."

"We're not here to enjoy ourselves." Bumble explained. She didn't like being in these kinds of places, it made her feel seedy.

"No ticket, no talking to the performers," said the lady, more business-like than a graph of facts in a faxed Filofax.

Nitsy could tell Bumble really wanted to get into this, so he quickly reached into his knapsack for his wallet. "We'll take two please. And can you change up a fifty for compliment slips?"

The person in the booth took the cash and handed back two tickets and a small book of paper slips of the design same as Nitsy had found earlier.

"Speak to Anxiety. She might have seen your friend," the lady confided.

Bumble and Nitsy made their way down the gloomy corridor, like lunch through a snake, all the while the music grew louder. It was the kind of generic dance beat that you could hang a tune on if you wanted, but no one had bothered.

They emerged in the main room, where the music was booming thanks to a DJ named Butterfingers who was dropping basslines all over the place. Even though it was the middle of the day the place was pretty full. Lonely people sat around at tables with those little candles on them, nodding along to the music. Their attention was focused on the stage at the far end of the room, where a young woman was leaning on a pole. Dressed in an overcoat, she was studiously avoiding the gazes of everyone in the room.

Not shy, Nitsy and Bumble grabbed a table near the stage. Nitsy ordered two bumbleberry juices from the passing waiter.

"You're enjoying this, aren't you?" Bumble whispered.

Nitsy shrugged. "It's nice to be out and about".

Bumble stood up and addressed the woman on the stage. "Anxiety?"

The woman didn't respond, but looked nervous at the attention.

"My partner and I are detectoring a series of strange things. Can we talk to you?" Bumble carried on.

"I'm in the middle of a dance," said Anxiety, turning away.

Bumble didn't get it; there wasn't a whole lot of dancing going on. Nitsy thrust into Bumble's hand the book of slips. She flicked through them. It was a selection of compliments such as 'Have you done something new with your hair?' and 'That top looks great on you'. Bumble tore off a 'You smell good'. Nitsy motioned for her to go ahead. Faster than a blender, Bumble stuffed the slip into Anxiety's coat pocket and sat back down again.

Anxiety checked her pocket and smiled when she read the slip. For the briefest of moments she made eye contact with Bumble. Nitsy slurped his bumbleberry juice through a straw. Bumble tore off another compliment slip and stuffed it into Anxiety's pocket. Nitsy tried to get her to pace herself, but Bumble was on a roll.

"You're enjoying this, aren't you?" said Nitsy.

Bumble went to deliver another compliment slip, but they had run out. Anxiety was now making her way across stage where a group of pie-chart makers were showering her with slips. Before

Nitsy could stop her, Bumble bounded straight onto the stage and whispered into Anxiety's ear.

Nitsy noticed the bouncers at the door stir and make their way to stop the intruder. Anxiety's face fell as Bumble spoke to her. She signalled to the DJ to stop the music. Butterfingers was happy to oblige -she so rarely got to play her sample of a record scratch finish.

* * *

Nitsy and Bumble waited in the dressing room as Anxiety got changed out of her overcoat and into her underwear.

"I'm a lingerie model mostly," she explained, "I only do the neurotic dancing to earn some extra compliments."

Nitsy and Bumble looked surprised.

"No one tells lingerie models they're hot because they think they must hear it all the time," Anxiety explained. It was enough to make the Detectors feel quite sorry for the woman. "Who's the peanut?" she asked.

"This is Nitson von Nitzenjammer," waved Bumble, "and I'm Bumblerumpskin."

"I'm afraid I can't tell you much about your dead professor friend," said Anxiety not at all anxiously. "The other night was the first time I'd seen him in here. I remember thinking he was part of the crunk-jazz fusion band on account of his trumpet case."

"He had his trumpet with him?" Nitsy asked.

"Yeah, I figured he was trying to sell the thing. There was a guy who came over to sit with him."

"What guy?" Bumble countered.

"I dunno, some guy. He didn't pay. The lads on the door kicked him out. Well after they'd got the stones out of their shoes." Anxiety grabbed her bag, ready to leave for the night.

"Pebblefoot," whispered Nitsy gravely.

"Don't you hate it when that happens?" said the neurotic dancer-hyphen-lingerie model.

Nitsy nodded sombrely.

"Are you sure that this other guy wasn't trying to take the trumpet from the professor?" Bumble suggested.

Anxiety shook her head.

"He took it out of the case and they even got as far as counting out the money. Then they got into some disagreement. I thought they were going to make a robust fisticuff salad, but then the bouncers kicked the other fellow out."

Bumble's head was reeling like a reel to reel tape machine recording the sound of a whole room of fishing reels. Could Professor Candlewick really have been ready to hand over his invention to Phantom Pebblefoot of all people?

The change in the Detectors' mood was lost on Anxiety, who was heading for the door. "Is it raining out? Will I need an umbrella?"

Without thinking Nitsy mumbled, "Just until the evening. Then we can all look forward to a westerly mild front."

It annoyed Bumble when her colleague displayed his meteorological knowledge.

Anxiety's face lit up. "That's where I know you from, peanutman! Channel 62 weather!"

Nitsy shifted ickily and looked into the far corner of the room. "Um, no."

"Yes! You're Clement Weatherfront. You wear citrus tie-pins, like, all the time. My flatmate and I watch out for the limes." Anxiety was as joyful as a smiley train on happy tracks.

"I think you've got me mistaken for someone else you mad neurotic temptress," Nitsy waffled with a mouthful of tongue.

Anxiety picked up an umbrella. "You know your clouds, Clement. Umbrella it is." Anxiety strode out of the door.

Oddly there was still a little anxiety left in the room. Bumble stared daggers, or at least very sharp letter openers, at Nitsy.

Anxiety reappeared at the door just to chirp "I hope you solve the case of the guy and the thing." Then she was gone.

Bumble strapped her wet squirrel to her head. "Come on," she prompted. "Sorry", she added, "I meant to say come on Clement Doodlebug. Thing. Whatever."

Nitsy traipsed out after her.

5

CLEMENT WEATHERFRONT

Nitsy had lost his job at the wall factory. This was the long, hot winter of the year the Detectors had practiced their noble art to bring to justice the vermin killer of farmacist Ms Penelope Loveslice. The height of the duo's popularity had undoubtedly been marked by their appearance on *Cuppa Tea and a Bit of Toast*, Channel 62's flagship magazine breakfast show. Taking time out to sit on that famous beige sofa had been no problem at all for Bumble, who had been able to knock out her piece on achieving sudden fame on her Pineapple ShinyBook in the cab on the way to the studio. Nitsy on the other hand was running out of excuses for his continued absences from the wall factory.

He'd had a cold for the *Hiya!* interview, flu for the *Pret a Nugget* opening and then something he'd decided to call a 'fluold', which coincidently occurred at exactly the same time as the Leicester Square premiere of *Upstairs Downstairs 2: The Quickening*. His bosses at the factory were becoming suspicious that whenever Nitsy was ill someone who looked very much like him was appearing at all sorts of public events. They warned him that no one could be that immunely challenged and still expect to carve out a successful career in wall manufacture. In short he was on thinner ice than someone standing on a frozen stoat wee.

Still, when he and Bumble got the invite to appear on *Cuppa Tea* to discuss 'this new thing called detectoring', Nitsy decided that one more day off couldn't hurt. Before they knew it they were sitting clammy under those studio lights talking to everybody's favourite morningtime faces, *CTAABOT* hosts Nick Biscuit and Jemimah Chaffinch. Nitsy enjoyed the whole thing (especially the pastries, which were FREE), but found himself too overwhelmed to generate much answer coverage for Nick and Jem. Thank goshness then for Bumble, who was witty and urban, a street poet waxing spherically on the art of detectoring and the timely arrest of a mouse at a farmacist shop.

For the most part Nitsy just sat there and smiled. He was regretting telling his employers at the wall factory to 'stick their job in a dark room' (even then they had said there was plenty of chance for Nitsy to advance in wall management, but he needed to actually go to work. Nitsy had replied that no one even wanted pre-fabricated walls anymore, that the real future lay in bricks and walls that could be built where buildings were actually going to be, and not inside another building on some industrial estate in Brackham-on-the-Bit. That's where he'd really lost them. Wall people don't like to hear too much about bricks, they lose all perspective. They told him they would forward his P45 and his desk tidy, which they didn't have to do as it was actually company property).

Nitsy was feeling pretty confident after the *Cuppa Tea* segment. Granted, he'd not said much and he'd lost his phone but the extra publicity was bound to be good for him and Bumble. It would likely lead to an increased interest in detectoring and probably open up the possibility of some kind of consultancy work. He soon realised that the reality was less rosy than a thorn. The phone stopped ringing (Nitsy had been trying his own number and had finally got through to someone who sounded like the weather channel through liver. Then the phone died. The irony that even Nitsy had stopped calling himself wasn't lost on him). In the end there was no consultancy, just some utility bills that needed paying and a fridge that refused to grow its own bumbleberries.

Nitsy swallowed his pride and went back to the wall factory. He found it was closing down. Apparently they were shifting their entire operation over to brick production. His old workmates explained this was all the suggestion of some bright spark and that it would cost the town of Brackham-on-the-Bit 1,500 jobs. Nitsy left the picket line quickly and quietly.

He signed up with a temping agency, writing temporary scores for films. That soon came to an end when they realised that no one heard the temp scores so they didn't really need to pay anyone to write one. Luckily for Nitsy that job led to an interview for something completely different at none other than the Channel 62 studios. It turned out that *Cuppa Tea and a Bit of Toast* were suddenly lacking a weather presenter after the last chap had accidentally choked on a Pineapple 6 left on the pastry table by some thoughtless guest. Nick Biscuit and Jemimah Chaffinch, for all their apparent unflappability, were quite useless and could only watch as the weatherchap expired on the studio floor with a ringtone dancing in his lungs. Anyway, his misfortune was Nitsy's luck.

Of course Nitsy had no particular skill or experience in reading the weather. It had been an administrative mix up that he'd been put forward for the job. Really he was meant to be there to do filing. But Nitsy seemed to take to it quite naturally. Jem and Nick both agreed it was the most exciting and engaging weather reading the show had ever had. Nitsy signed off to the nation's cereal nibblers as Clement Weatherfront. There was a reason for this impulsive piece of random pseudonymery, though Nitsy only realised when they had gone to some adverts.

Whereas some folks would be unquestionably pleased at chancing their way into a weather presenting job, for Nitsy the fortune wasn't something he could share with everyone. He knew his partner Bumble hated quite passionately the weatherpeople. This all stemmed from an insect themed party she was due to have on her 7th birthday. Weatherchap of the day Jeff Tunasteak had predicted clear skies and sun drops as big as your head. Bumble's party had been set out perfectly in the garden and she had waited in costume and delirious anticipation for what was sure to be the most amazing day on the primary school calendar. The weather turned out to be awful. It thundered like dustbins going down the hill. It hailed like legionnaires at Caesar's foot. The wind whipped up like meringue. Essentially the whole day was ruined. Bumble had recounted the whole miserable tale to Nitsy years later, how for her little 7 year old self there was no comeback for the ruined day. The only person remotely accountable was Jeff Tunasteak, who'd got the whole thing very wrong. And hold him accountable she did, a feeling which turned over the years into a deep suspicion and dislike of all those who stood in front of a greenscreen and pointed at clouds that weren't there.

All of this occurred to Nitsy as he had been waving his hand over East Anglia. Bumble didn't even know about his sacking from the wall factory. If she knew he was now earning a living as what she called a 'drizzle plum' things could become quite impossible at home. As he neared the end of his report he knew he couldn't give his real name to the people at home or else he would be discovered. He opted for the jazzy, friendly sounding moniker Clement Weatherfront.

He was a hit with the viewers. Someone from East Anglia, who had been impressed with the sweep of Nitsy's hand, sent in a tie pin in the shape of some clementines, in honour of their new favourite weatherchap. This became quite the running gag as people sent in tie pins from all over the country, tuning in to see if Nitsy would be wearing theirs and what he had to say about the coming days.

The only problem with this was the likelihood that Bumble would one day find out about Nitsy's filthy little secret and that he was no longer working at the wall factory. He reasoned to himself though that at home they usually watched *Whoops! Dinosaur Poo!* on CBeebles in the mornings, so Nitsy reasoned this would never ever be an issue they would ever have to face ever.

6

AIR BUMBLELEGS

"Right," said Nitsy. "So where are we?"

Bumble was looking in the bin. She raised an eyebrow and then her whole head to towards the sign above them that read 'Bus Stop'.

"I mean with the case," he said removing his hat. It had finally stopped raining. "If Candlewick was willing to sell the Thinking Man's Trumpet then why would Pebblefoot go and death him?"

"Don't know," Bumble shrugged.

"What if Pebblefoot had nothing to do with the theft from the museum? What if someone else killed the professor?"

Bumble shrugged again.

"Okay, what's the problem?"

"Isn't there some weather somewhere that needs reading?" The words tumbled out of Bumble's mouth like vended chocolate.

Nitsy nodded. Of course."I see," he said, because he saw, "That day when you were seven and the rain came along and ruined your wasp costume and all your friends had to go home. You know, I knew Jeff Tunasteak for fourteen seconds before he died with someone's phone -we'll never know whose- in his guts and he would have been horrified to learn that he inadvertently ruined a perfectly good seventh birthday party."

Bumble shook her head. "That's not it at all."

"No?"

"No. And it wasn't a wasp, I was dressed as a bumblebee. Anyway, I'm over all that now."

"Really? Because you still don't wear horizontal stripes."

Bumble sat down on the little rain specked plastic seat in the bus shelter. "It's not that you're selling yourself out to the Met Office, Nitsy. I knew we'd have to pay the rent somehow, but that's what I thought your job at the wall factory was for."

"Yeah, they kinda let me go from that one. What can you do, huh? Bricks."

"I thought you were all about the detectoring. I thought we both were. Then when I saw you with your crazy funky cool tie pins, laughing with Nick Biscuit and Jemimah Chaffinch, well, I realised that maybe our detectoring days were over. I've known for a while."

Nitsy was shocked to hear Bumble say such things. She was always the one who wore her detectoring badge on her sleeve (literally. She had patches sewn onto all of her clothes, even her pants. Even though not all of those had sleeves. But some did). "What are you saying? We should give up? What about the case?"

Bumble didn't like saying the words, but supposed she might as well say it all at once. "What case? No one asked us to Detector anything."

"No, but..."

"It's my fault. I was so happy to relive the glory days that I dragged us away from having our cup of coffee and reading the supplements."

"But Professor Candlewick is dead," said Nitsy.

"It's a job for the police, not us," said Bumble calmly.

"And what about the trumpet?"

"If it was Pebblefoot who stole it, and I'm beginning to think it wasn't, then what advantage does that give him? He wields the same powers of Projection anyhow and without looking like he's in a brass ensemble. The trumpet is useless."

To prove her point Bumble nodded towards the dustbin. Nitsy peered inside. A discarded copy of that day's local paper proclaimed:

'Bizarre Invention Recovered.
Police Hunt Pebblefoot.'

44

"They found the trumpet in the canal this morning," Bumble explained.

The 305 to 5th Avenue trundled up the road towards them. Bumble took off her squirrel hat. She gave it to Nitsy. "There is no detectoring mystery here, just a grubby little murder."

"What's this for?" he asked. Bumble didn't say anything. Nitsy gave it back. "It's your detectoring hat. It was my gift for solving the Loveslice case."

"That was a long time ago, Nits," said Bumble, "it's over. Let it go." She flagged down the bus.

"Where are you going?" Nitsy yelped.

"Home." The bus sang into the bus stop.

"Take the squirrel," Nitsy commanded.

"No. You wear it."

"I can't, I've already got a hat."

"Then wear both!"

"No! They're a set, that's the whole point! Now put it back on and let's go and find the next detectoring or whatever's cooking in your brain." He struggled to fit the hat back onto Bumble's head. They both bounced off the walls of the bus stop.

"There's nothing cooking."

"You don't fool me Bumble. I know when there's a brainstorm going on in there."

"You're wrong. And in any case I've got a mindbrella, so get off!"

Bumble pushed Nitsy backwards and he fell into the bin. The bus was making its way off down the road.

Bumble started off, running after the double-decker. Nitsy dragged himself out of the rubbish to follow her. Then at the corner of his eyes the world flashed dark. He called out after Bumble, but she was way off in the distance and almost caught up with the retreating bus.

Nitsy put his best foot to the floor and started to run. He didn't even make it half a step before an awful pain shot up from his left big toe, all the way up to his right eyebrow. With a scream he dropped to the floor.

* * *

Bumble flew Air Bumblelegs after that bus. She tried calling after the driver but there were several tonnes of steel and glass between the two of them so communication was difficult. She realised that Nitsy was not hot on her tail. She glanced back at the bus stop and saw him having a little sit down on the pavement. He had taken the whole end of detectoring thing quite badly. But sitting on your bum at a bus stop, well that was the protest of a small child. She reasoned to herself that they would have all the time in the world to talk when they both got home. She promised herself that she would get home first and put the kettle on. With this thought Bumble found new reserves of energy and was propelled ever closer to the door of the bus. She was now running so fast it felt like she was flying. The driver finally noticed her and slowed to let her on. Breathless, she fiddled in her purse for the exact change.

* * *

Nitsy tried again to get off the ground. Every time he got to his feet, the pain would return and send him quickly back earthwards. The sky seemed to be getting darker and there was a chill in the air that was less cold and more a feeling of dread. Nitsy knew he was very much in trouble. He shouted in vain for Bumble, but she and the bus had disappeared from view. Frantically Nitsy crawled along the pavement, but he was gripped by the ever-present feeling of there being some kind of stone or pebble digging into his foot. It was then the shadow fell across Nitsy. All he could do then was to stare back into the eyes of his sedimentary sole tormentor.

* * *

The bus came to a halt at the end of the line. Bumble knew something was wrong when she looked out of the window. It looked nothing like her street. She turned to the driver.

"5th Avenue?" she enquired.

"Nah, you want the 305 for 5th Avenue," the driver sniffed.

"But this is the 305."

"This is the 5."

"No, it's the 305 for the 5th."

"No," the driver grimaced, "this is the 5 for the 305th."

Bumble looked outside again. It was misty out there, and it wasn't clear where there was. "When can I get back into town?"

"Tomorrow," the driver replied.

"Tomorrow?" Bumble croaked, "can't I come back with you now?"

"'Fraid not love. Going back to the depot." He pressed the switch and the doors hissed open. The mist wafted in, cold like when you're shopping for ice cream on a warm day. With no choice, Bumble stepped of the bus. It roared away behind her, leaving her alone in the opaque chill outside a shabby looking building. The filthy windows gave no clue as to its purpose, and the peeling paintwork suggested it had not been used for anything for quite some time. But faded letters on the hanging scraps of tattered awning over the doorway told Bumble where she had found herself.

It was the Erstwhile & Somewhen Farmacopeoia.

7

RETAIN YOUR SPORK

Picture if you will a pea that has fallen out of its bag in the freezer and has become frozen next to the ice cream you bought on that warm day. Picture that freezer in a locked room, under a mountain, inside a sturdy jiffy bag. That's how trapped Nitsy found himself to be. The last thing he remembered seeing was a used *Pret a Nugget* box blowing along the pavement outside the bus stop and the way it melted into darkness and fear. And he remembered hearing that Justine McTimblebaum song, but that was everywhere. At least the pain in his foot had gone. He'd had time enough in the small room he was in to thoroughly inspect his Trucks (he couldn't afford Vans) and find that, of course, there was no pebble in there at all. It was proof, if any were needed, that he was now in the clutches of the Phantom.

Nitsy had tried to find a way out of the cell. His Pineapple 6 had no signal, which left no chance of him being able to SMS, IM or ChumSpace Bumble. The door to the cell was immovably immovable, locked by some devilishly complicated mechanism such as a lock or maybe a chair wedged against the door handle on the outside. The lock itself looked accessible. Maybe there was a chance that Nitsy could pick it, if only he had the right tool. He searched his pockets. From what he could see he would need a long, thin implement with four prongs, one of which with a rounded edge. He was glad that he had kept the spork he got with his cheese salad yesterday. He ruffled through his pocket, but turned up only the standard stainless steel fork he used as a mobile back scratcher. It would be quite hopeless as a lock pick. Perhaps he would be able to grind one of the edges down into a sporklike curve given a bit of effort.

From everywhere there suddenly sounded a voice. It filled the room like awkwardness in a busy lift.

"If only you were wearing your other jacket," said the voice, thick like oil.

"Phantom? I know it's you," said Nitsy trying not to sound fearful.

"I can read your thoughts, young Nitson," came the reply.

51

"Alright, what am I thinking now?"

"You're thinking 'I wonder how he'll answer this question'," said the Phantom. You could practically hear him smirking. Nitsy put away his back scratcher. The Phantom continued, "and now you are thinking on what I have in store for you. How I will dispatch you from the world. What evil awaits you in the eye of my twisted mind."

"Actually I was rather wishing I'd retained the spork I'd used to eat my salad yesterday. But it seems I left it in my other jacket." Nitsy was fairly sure he came off in a cool, collected kind of way. Maybe even a bit swag, a good effort considering all he could taste was peril.

"Um, that's what I meant by the comment about the jacket", said the Phantom, "it was a reference to the, uh, spork thing."

"Oh," said Nitsy, feeling stupid.

"Not so clever without your partner, are you?" The Phantom was trying to taunt Nitsy.

A thought popped into Nitsy's mind. He'd already checked his jacket pockets, but he somehow understood that if he checked again he knew he would find what he needed to pick the lock. And just like that he retrieved from his pocket a shiny new spork. Amazing, always the last place you look again. Stealthily he moved towards the lock and set to work.

"You've both been quite tenacious in your pursuit of me," said the Phantom. "At least you were warmer than those foolish police. They're only just getting back from Cheddar Gorge as we speak."

Nitsy worked quickly at the lock, aligning the tumblers with the edge of the spork. Only one more stood between him and escape.

"You forget who you're dealing with, Nitson," teased the Phantom. "Are you sure that is a spork in your hand? Or is it just... a projection?"

Nitsy froze. The spork in his hand had turned into a receipt from *Much Ado About Muffins*. The Phantom had been toying with him.

"Ha ha ha ha!" Phantom Pebblefoot chuckled at his cunning deception.

Nitsy shouted back at the laughter, "what do you want with me? I'm just a humble wallmaker turned regional weatherman who had a brief moment in the spotlight and was contracted for a time by Hotpoint. I'm nothing special. I'm of no use to you."

"On the contkertree Nitson, you are precisely the person whose help I require," the Phantom intoned seriously. Nitsy severely doubted that little slice of ruse, a suspicion the Phantom picked up on. "You are aware of the circumstances surrounding the theft of Professor Candlewick's trumpet?"

Nitsy nodded.

"Then you know I had no cause to either steal what I already possessed and could otherwise afford. And that I had no cause to kill the man."

"Then who did?" demanded Nitsy, an entirely pertinent question.

"Philbert Drak."

Nitsy shook his head. That was impossible. "He doesn't exist anymore. He's gone."

"I assure you that Philbert Drak is very much among us," said the Phantom.

Nitsy shivered. "Don't say that name. He was banished to Nothing for all time. There's no way He Who Shall No Longer Be CC'd could have anything to do with this."

"He may have taken a different form," the Phantom conceded, "but you know as well as I that Drak's hunger for dominion over All is as enduring as the rocks in the sea or a Christmas song from the 70's. There is nothing that can dissuade him from his plan and it is a very involved plan."

Nitsy thought on this. For some reason he found himself entertaining the jumbled thought of fishing reels being recorded. Strangely it reminded him of Bumble and he suddenly hoped she was safe and warm with a cup of tea. "Have his plans included a corduroy wearing mouse assassin?" Nitsy asked. "And by that I mean a mouse who assassins people, not a person who assassins mouses," he added as clarification.

"Yes."

"I knew it", said Nitsy with a shake of his fist. "But why are you telling me all this?"

"Because I need your help, young Nitson."

"Ha! Phantom Pebblefoot needs my help. That's a ha of laughter by the way, meaning I find the whole concept laughable. I might have actually believed you for a second, but it's just another one of your tricksy projections isn't it? You're enjoying messing with my melon aren't you, you sicko?"

"It is the truth", the Phantom spoke earnestly, "and you must listen to me as we haven't much time."

"Time for what?"

"To stop the machinations of Philbert Drak before he escapes his cell of Nothing to conquer All!" The Phantom's voice echoed off the walls, carving a sonic sculpture of doom in Nitsy's ears before shattering into several million pieces of panic and entering the Detector's bloodstream. At least that's what it felt like.

"You want to stop Drak? Your mentor? What kind of minty are you?" Nitsy babbled, overcome.

"Drak is a polemist of evil. Some of us are happy to cut a rug in the world as it is, but he's one of these dark hearted souls who can't see any middle ground. If he was to have his way then I would be cast aside as everyone else would be. I may be a little slippery, a little nefarious but in the eyes of Philbert Drak I belong with all the other scum like you. No offence."

"No, cheers for that. That really makes me feel good," said Nitsy. "How am I supposed to stop Drak?"

"Leave that to me," whispered the Phantom in a scheming kind of way, "all I need is for you and your partner to find him."

"Me and...?"

"Your colleague Bumblerumpskin."

"Ah," said Nitsy, "bit of a thing there. She's kind of moved on from the detectoring world."

"Moved on?" the Phantom repeated incredulously. "Young Nitson, do you not understand that it is the fate of the world we are talking about here? Drak is skilfully executing his plan as we speak."

"Yeah, but Bumble's had an offer to take over writing the crossword for the Tribune?" said Nitsy, with an emphasis on the end of his sentence? Which suggested a question? But actually wasn't? But is nonetheless the speaking style of our times? "I think she's quite excited as potentially she could be filling it in correctly every day."

There was no answer from the Phantom. Outside the cell clattered a rush of oncoming footsteps. A key turned in the lock. Nitsy steadied himself, armed in one hand with his backscratcher and in the other with a receipt for two gingerbread lattes and a tiffin slice. The door swung open. For the first time in plain, lucid sight, and reasonable lighting, Nitsy found himself face to face with the Phantom. He was so-so. Underneath the fedora and long coat Nitsy could see he had a fairly aggressive dry skin condition.

He was also quite worked up.

"Imagine someone whose will to rule the world cannot even be muted by their being removed from existence. Imagine someone who could turn an unsuspecting man into a mouse and force him to steal and death a lady. Imagine someone so insidiously powerful that he can somehow arrange for the theft of the Thinking Man's Trumpet, do another death on the professor who made it and not only get away with it, but make the authorities believe that somebody else, me, was responsible for those crimes. Can you imagine that you drippy little Detector?"

Nitsy had a go.

"Stop!" yelled the Phantom. "You don't have to imagine it! It's happening already, that's the entire point!"

"Yeah, but they found the trumpet this morning. So problem solved," Nitsy shrugged.

The Phantom collected himself. "The policemen have it?"

"It was in the canal. A bit wet because it was out of its case, but it's safe and sound."

The Phantom gulped. This made Nitsy nervous. The Phantom slumped down in the corner, which didn't help Nisty's nerves.

"Oh dear. This is quite possibly worse than I originally imagined," the Phantom sighed.

"What...", Nitsy began. The rest of his sentence fell on the floor.

From the wall against which the Phantom sat, a dozen hands emerged. Some pinned him fast, while some rifled through his pockets. He struggled.

"Help!" he cried.

Nitsy pounced into action. Well in his mind he did, but in reality he found himself glued to the spot.

"I said help me!" the Phantom gagged. One hand took from his pocket the keys to the cell.

"I can't move" Nitsy shouted.

Another hand popped out of the floor near the door and gave it a little tap.

"The door," the Phantom said, "the door."

Nisty pulled and strained but he was as static as an aerial-less television in a static caravan. The door slammed shut. A moment later the hands released the Phantom and disappeared back into the wall. The cell was quiet.

"Why didn't you do anything?" asked the Phantom, standing up and adjusting his hat.

"What time is it?" asked Nitsy.

"Just after midnight. What does that have to do with anything?"

"It's Sunday," said Nitsy. He hung his head. "I won't be able to move for another 24 hours."

The Phantom kicked the wall. "Drak!"

"Did you see those hands?" Nitsy murmured, "They came out of nowhere."

"Not nowhere, Nothing. Drak was onto me the whole time. He knew I was trying to recruit you and your partner. And now we're trapped."

"Cheese's crust!", said Nitsy.

The Phantom sat down again. He squinted at Nitsy. "Is your hat a squirrel eating a peanut?" he asked.

"It's a set. I'm just holding on to one for someone," replied Nitsy with a cough.

Then they were both quiet.

"Go back to your side of the room," said the Phantom all of a sudden. Nitsy did a double take, he hadn't moved.

"Hello? I'm frozen in a Sunday, I can't move?" Nitsy sang. "But if you think you're going to creep up on me you've got another thing coming. You go and sit back on your side of the room."

"Listen here you inanimate Detector," the Phantom rasped, "I know you're just pretending you can't move, but you're closer to me than you were two minutes ago and I haven't budged an inch."

"I'll have you know my condition is very real thank you very much," Nitsy shrilled. "But I wouldn't put it past you to start projecting into my melon that the room is shrinking just for your own deviant pleasure,"

The Phantom jumped to his feet. Nitsy flinched, well as much as he could flinch. The Phantom started circling the room, examining the walls.

"What are you doing?"

The Phantom tapped the wall. "You feel like the room is shrinking. I feel like the room is shrinking. There are only two possibilities. One..."

"The room is shrinking," Nitsy offered.

"Or two. Someone is making us both think that the room is shrinking. Most likely with the Projected thought of awkwardness in a crowded lift."

Nitsy bug-eyed the walls. Were they closing in or was it all in his mind?

"The Drak one is still close by. Possibly on the other side of that wall. He isn't finished with us yet," the Phantom whispered.

Nitsy's voice shook, "w-w-what will he do to us?"

"If the room really is shrinking then we will be crushed," said the Phantom. Fear jumped out of Nitsy's face in the shape of an unattractive gurn. The Phantom gave a second possibility, "But if we are both being subjected to a Drak Projection, we'll tear each other apart with awkward paranoia."

"I don't like the sound of either of those," said Nitsy.

The Phantom came up close to Nitsy. He was trying to be friendly and reassuring, but it was difficult to feel comforted by someone who seemed to exist in permanent shadow and who had a name like the Phantom. Still, Nitsy gave the guy a break.

"I wouldn't put either past him. But if I know Drak, and we've summered together on several occasions so I think I do, the closing walls are a Projection," said the Phantom. "What we must do is to try and not let it overrun our minds and vegetablise us with fear and paranoia."

"How?" Nitsy asked.

"You need to Detector things. Lots of things. Lots of really good things. A stream of excellent detectorings will act as a sort of mindbrella to the Projection."

"Then what?"

"Then we have to hope that your partner finds us in time," said the Phantom, not really sounding like he believed in the likelihood of that happening.

Nitsy sensed the Phantom's lack of conviction and knew he had to remain positive. "Bumble will be here. She'll be wondering where I am and she will find us. If she's had her dinner."

The Phantom nodded, still unconvinced.

"Joining the three points on equal distances on three dimensions drawn from the corner of a room will give you a triangle," Nitsy exclaimed.

The Phantom arched an eyebrow. Then he realised what Nitsy was doing.

"Noses are strange," Nitsy observed. "You could make toasted paninis with an iron. This room smells a bit like wee. Your hat looks like something from an old film."

To the Phantom the room appeared to have stopped shrinking. Nitsy could tell it was working, so he stepped up his game.

"Some people call hazelnuts Philberts. Why don't we fall out of bed when we're sleeping? Don't dust mites look like croissants?"

On he went, detectoring as though his life depended on it. Because it did. Drak had them within his grasp and the unlikely team of Nitson von Nitzenjammer and Phantom Pebblefoot were running out of time.

8

ERSTWHILE & SOMEWHEN FARMACOPEOIA

Penelope Loveslice's now legendary farmacy, the Erstwhile & Somewhen Farmacopeoia, came from humble beginnings. Back in the days when being a farmacist didn't even exist as a profession, a teenaged Penelope started earning pocket money by hand rearing many of the elemental notions that we now use everyday. It's difficult to appreciate how far reaching and revolutionary her work was, seeing as we now take it for granted. You would probably be surprised to learn that she was the first person to introduce déjà vu to the world. She discovered it while backpacking through treacle and thought, quite insightfully, that people everywhere would get a little kick from thinking they'd done before what they were just now doing. She began to farm it in large volumes and it would literally fly out the door of the lock-up she rented from a farmer who was supportive of the young entrepreneur's work.

Déjà vu was a success again and again. But Penelope wasn't one to sit on her laurels, not when there was an entire planet of people's minds to populate with her wares. You know when you realise you've been staring at something for quite a while and then catch yourself and feel a bit foolish for it and can't even see what you were really thinking about that whole time? Penelope discovered that. She called it Zoningout, and people use it all the time, though they don't always remember.

It wasn't just the discovery of these elements that made Penelope a success. No, that was just the start. She soon found that many of these things could be combined. There are only so many elements in the Notional Table, just as there are only so many elements in the Periodic Table, but it is possible to create entirely new compounds by mixing them up. Have you ever had déjà vu that you were staring into space thinking about something? That's an original Loveslice compound of déjà vu and Zoningout. Ever had déjà vu that seemed to go on for way too long, even to the point where you have time to tell the person sat next to you "this is weird, I've got déjà vu and it's still going on. I feel I've already said that. And that. And that"? That is a compound of two parts

65

déjà vu (DV) to one part of Longday (L). Loveslice gave us the formula:

$$DV_2L_1$$

The permutations and possibilities were endless. A new science hadn't been born, because it wasn't a science. However, many regarded Penelope Loveslice as the Newton figure of the thought world and an important name in the creation of detectoring. The Thought Kitchen, the world's leading College of Detectoring, was founded on the principles she discovered. She became a poster child for student Detectors, especially for one Bumblerumpskin who did indeed have a poster of Loveslice on her wall at college, next to her poster of Four Nice Boysingers.

When the bus had left her outside the Erstwhile & Somewhen Farmacopeoia, Bumble had been saddened to see this symbol of Loveslice's life's work in its current state. Since its owner had died the doors had been boarded up and 'For Sale' signs now plastered the building. It wasn't what you wanted to happen to the magical shop you'd been reading about all your life. That's what Bumble had been thinking as she stood staring aimlessly at the door, that and the remarkable fact that it looked very much like Harrods. It was then that the door had swung open. Bumble knew it would be a foolish thing to venture inside alone and it would be considered trespassing. But all the time it had been trading, she had only visited the Erstwhile & Somewhen Farmacopeoia once and that was only to use the toilet. She had been a child and she had needed somewhere to be sick that afternoon. Now, as a grown up, she had always felt that even if she could get past the reverence she had for the place, to see it for real would make her heart pop with joy. When Penelope had died it looked like no one would ever set foot in the place again. Now Bumble found herself in front of an open door into the most fascinating and amazing place in the world. It would be silly to pass up the opportunity, wouldn't it?

Inside, the Farmacopeoia was massive. Rows and rows of aisles stretched off into the distance. They went left and right, up and down, forwards and backwards. It was insanely big. And the shelves. You couldn't count the number of shelves in one aisle, let alone all of them. Each was stocked to the limits, bowing under the weight of ideas, notions and emotions. Bumble started to feel weak at the knees at the infinity of it all, at the wonderful possibilities.

What if you were the world's most passionate artist, who poured themselves fully into every sketch or painting that they did? What if you saw not a pencil in your hand but a dozen, two dozen, compositions of anything your mind could conjure? What if you went to an art shop that stocked over one million pencils? That is the kind of infinite potential Bumble felt as she walked through the Erstwhile & Somewhen Farmacopeoia.

Finally, she understood why Penelope Loveslice had relocated her store to where she had. The old lockup she'd once used had quickly become defunct; it couldn't store the new elements she was discovering everyday. She had rented some high street retail unit in Brackham-on-the-Bit town centre for a while, but the rates were so high. Again, the space soon filled up with the growing range. Penelope decided she would have to move again, but that it should be for the last time. The problem was that nowhere had anywhere near the space to accommodate her operation. In the end Penelope leased not a place, but a place in time. There were lots of property options in the past you see, because no one lived there anymore. The only downside to moving to a moment in the past would be that her shop would only be accessible to people in the present by means of a special bus. Penelope shrewdly predicted that this wouldn't be problem as most of her custom was specialist trade. She wasn't exactly running the kind of business that relied on passing trade like your *Pret a Nugget* or your *We Have Stationery* or your *Much Ado About Muffins.*

The move gave Penelope the space to fulfil her vision for the Farmacopeoia to become the largest repository of thoughts and feelings in the world. So how big was the Erstwhile & Somewhen Farmacopeoia? It was as big as Harrods. Specifically, it was as big as Harrods was at five past three on October 15th 1994. For some reason property prices in the 90's were comparatively cheap.

Bumble was surprised to run into anyone in such a large place. Even if it had been open and filled with hundreds of shoppers, she imagined she would have a hard time meeting another soul. She'd been wandering for hours and she was still only near the entrance close to the tube station. If she wanted to visit the gift shop she would need to go to the third floor, said the store directory. If she wanted to eat in the Farmacopeoia's Sushi Bar she would need travel all the way over to the basement. If she was to be honest (and she could tell whether or not she was telling herself the truth) Bumble was a little nonplussed by the place. It was too big. There were too many possibilities and things to look at that she felt she could never get it all done. And if you knew you couldn't get it all done, then why start in the first place? She felt like the tear of a drop in an ocean of oceans.

It was cold in the aisles. The heating to the shop must have been turned off a long time ago. Bumble wished she still had her squirrel hat. Then that made her think about Nitsy and their exchange at the bus stop. Bumble felt bad that she'd dismissed detectoring in such a way. Nitsy had looked crushed. Really Bumble was ever still the die-hard Detector she had always been. It was just so difficult to hang on to the art in a world of sceptics and non-believers. The recent episode with the trumpet had brought home to Bumble why they had never been able to earn a living as Detectors. No one took them or the art seriously. So as much as she was inspired walking in the Erstwhile & Somewhen Farmacopeoia, the fact that it was hidden away from reality in a quiet afternoon in 1994 confirmed to Bumble that detectoring wasn't something that belonged in the real world.

She stopped at a display of daydreams, which were marked as on special offer. What was the point of daydreams anyhow? As Bumble picked one up she thought back to all the daydreams she could remember having. She could only conclude they were useless as they stopped you from doing something practical while you were having them and then they never came true anyway.

"They're buy one get one free," said a lady behind her. Bumble nearly dropped her daydream. She hurriedly put it back on the shelf.

69

"The door was open. I'm sorry, I'll go," she volunteered.

"No, stay," said the lady, "I've put the kettle on." Bumble recognised a smell, a perfume. She had smelled it before. She turned and couldn't believe her eyes. There, not nine cereal bar lengths in front of her, was Penelope Loveslice. She looked quite good for a dead person. She radiated the kind of warmth and wisdom that makes someone quite attractive. Some call it Lovelysexymagic.

"Of all people I should be glad to share a cup of tea with you, Bumble," said Penelope with a smile. Bumble didn't have the chance to reply as Penelope led them off down the aisle towards the break room. And there, over a table, doilies and some strong tea, Bumble got the chance to speak to the ghost of her all-time number one farmacist heroine.

9

ENIGMA BITCH

Bumble couldn't look Penelope Loveslice in the
eye. This was in part due to the translucent nature of the
Farmacist's apparition, but mainly it was down to Bumble feeling
humbled.

It was strange to Bumble that she found herself having tea with
this woman. Those lucky enough to meet one's heroes often only
get to do so once and it can be an odd experience to greet in person
that face that has sat for so long next to Harry Boysinger's above

one's bed. For Bumble the encounter was made even stranger in that a) the woman was dead and b) Bumble had already met her when she was dead and had even been involved in solving the case of her murder. Honestly it made for a bit of a muddle, but at least Bumble felt she had something to bring the conversation table.

Penelope had been hugely thankful for Bumble's efforts in tracking her killer. She'd asked how the detectoring was going? This was a question Bumble dreaded considering recent events and her lack of faith in the whole matter. She'd cagily described the case of the Thinking Man's Trumpet and Phantom Pebblefoot, but let it sort of tail off into vagueness at the part when the case was abandoned because her disillusion and self doubt had manifested as a disproportionate grievance with her colleague who had been moonlighting as a weatherman. Penelope wouldn't let it drop though, dammit.

"So then what happened?" she had asked pointedly, while pouring them both a third cup of tea. Bumble stalled and made some sounds like 'uh', 'erm' and 'brrriiing, pung, pow'. Penelope just sat there and waited. It was awful. Eventually Bumble had admitted to throwing in the towel of detectoring.

"But you're ever so good at it my dear," Penelope had said.

That had been a little boost for Bumble, until she remembered who she was talking to; this amazing person who'd created an entire field of thought and built up one of the biggest businesses in the world. Suddenly her problems seemed rather tiny.

By their fifth cup of tea (and a second trip to the little Detector's room for Bumble), conversation had turned to

Penelope. Although she was dead she still had to stick around for a while to tie up a few loose ends. "Administration," she'd explained. She was looking to pass on the deeds for the Farmacopeoia onto a reputable party, ideally one with an interest in thought and detectoring. It had taken a long while to find someone who wasn't a pie-chart maker who wanted to simply turn the place into a theme park.

"Thankfully I believe I have found the right chap," said Penelope. "And as soon as the deal is done I can finally shuffle off for a rest."

Bumble smiled, but it wasn't a real smile. Penelope looked her over.

"Come out from the mindbrella dear," she soothed.

Bumble tumbled her eyeballs like she didn't know what Penelope was talking about.

"Come out from the mindbrella," Penelope coaxed. "Take a walk in the mindstorm."

Bumble looked unsure.

"Trust in your detectoring," Penelope continued. "Let yourself see what you already know."

Bumble finished her tea. Inside her mind she allowed the mindstorm to scramble into new heights. It blew away the tedium of her job and the beige anaesthesia of *Cuppa Tea and a Bit of Toast*. Somewhere inside a little fence blew over, battered by the mindstorm. The boundary gone, thoughts began to fly at her. Bumble suddenly saw that you could cut cheese with scissors-there was no reason you couldn't, that a scratching hoover would be called a scratchuver, that *Whoops! Dinosaur Poo!* was unquestionably the most brilliant thing on TV, that if she had a PA he'd be named Honey Notes, that the Thinking Man's Trumpet had been recovered without its case, that a year ago an awful lot of brass fasteners had been stolen by that mouse.

"Philbert Drak!" Bumble cried.

"There it is," nodded Penelope. She sipped her tea. Bumble's attention was elsewhere; her mind was a hurricane of detectorings.

"The trumpet is a projector, the last thing a Projector would need or want," Bumble spelled out, "But nobody wanted the trumpet in the first place."

Penelope punched the air, "Go on dear, bring it home!"

Bumble took a deep breath and hoped her mouth could keep up with her thoughts. "Professor Candlewick invented the trumpet as way to give non-Projectors the power to project thoughts into people's minds, right? You have to ask, who out there would be the last person to benefit from such a levelling of abilities?"

"Phantom Pebblefoot." answered Penelope.

"No," said Bumble. "That's what I thought. That's not to say the Phantom didn't want the trumpet. We know he tried to buy it from the Professor, but his interest was further reaching than protecting the exclusivity of his power."

Penelope leaned forward in her chair.

"Phantom Pebblefoot has been the most feared figure on the Drak side since Philbert Drak was imprisoned in Nothing. What does everyone know about Drak? That he is an unstoppable wrong 'un. Why, since he's been in prison he has engineered fourteen escape attempts. In twelve of them he got as far as getting a train ticket before being caught. The guy is serious news."

"Oh yes," Penelope concurred. "Well he arranged to have me killed so of course I'd agree."

"When news of the trumpet broke, Drak must have sensed the opportunity had arrived for him to finally escape."

"But you said nobody ever wanted the trumpet," said Penelope, confused.

"The case, Drak wanted the trumpet case."

Bumble fumbled in her bag. She produced the newspaper supplement with the Darius Candlewick article.

"Candlewick spent years building that trumpet. After all that he wanted to make sure it wouldn't get damaged so he built a custom carry case for it." She pointed at the picture of the purple suede trumpet case. Penelope craned in to see.

"Only this is no ordinary case," Bumble explained. "Not only does it protect the trumpet, but it repairs it if it ever gets damaged. See, here."

Bumble picked out the line in the article and read, "dents, scuffs or scratches are ironed out while the trumpet is in the case, explains Candlewick. The repair facility is almost as remarkable as the trumpet itself. We have even carried out tests wherein we completely disassembled the trumpet, blew it up and ran over the pieces with a sit on lawnmower. Even in that extreme state of disrepair the case was still able to reconfigure the brass junk into a fully functioning thought Projecting trumpet."

"Oh, that's clever." Penelope nodded.

"It's clever, but it's also frickin' dangerous!" Bumbled proclaimed. "You wouldn't even need to know how to put one together; the trumpet case would make a trumpet for you. All you would need is to fill it with some raw material."

"Like a few hundred brass fasteners, stolen from We Have Stationery several years ago," Penelope gasped.

"Exactly," Bumble nodded gravely. "Whoever possesses the trumpet case could have as many trumpets as they could create. Enough for an entire army. Drak has been planning this for years. He even came up with a fall guy in the shape of one P. Pebblefoot."

Bumble leaned back in her chair, as satisfied as she would be had she eaten a long tube of cannelloni. Then another thought bubbled in her brain.

"The only thing Drak failed to do was to stop our investigation," she mused. Then with horror she shrieked, "Nitsy! We have to find Nitsy, I think he may be in trouble."

Penelope was on her feet in an instant. Well, not really because she didn't have much in the way of feet, she more sort of tapered off at the legs. But she led Bumble quickly to the escalator, which they rode all the way into the basement. They whisked past the stock rooms, right into the deepest recesses of the Farmacopeoia. Penelope opened a door with a wave of her hand and turned on the lights by waving the other.

"This is Darius Candlewick's first invention. The most advanced detectoring computer in the world," Penelope declared.

In the room Bumble beheld a Commodore 64.

Penelope switched it on. They waited a while for the program to boot from the tape drive.

"So, you're dead then?" Bumble puffed, "what's that like?"

Penelope shrugged. "S'alright."

Eventually, DetectoringWorks 1.4 was ready to go. "Just type in your colleague's name and the computer will search for him." explained Penelope.

Bumble typed in 'Nitson von Nitzenjammer' and pressed return. There was another long wait as the computer carried out the search. To pass the time the two of them sang that Justine McTimblebaum song that was everywhere at the moment. Then the computer pinged. The search results read: 'Not Found.'

Bumbled typed in 'Nitsy'. The computer instantly came back with 'Found: Nitsy'. The screen changed to an image of Nitsy. He was frozen in position. There was no sound, but it looked like he was speaking in tongues. He was concentrating very hard and Bumble could tell he was in a bit of a panic.

"Oh no," said Bumble. "He's trapped in Sunday again."

A figure paced past Nitsy on the screen. Bumble jumped. It was Phantom Pebblefoot. What was he doing with Nitsy?

"Calm down dear," Penelope said, "they're both of them imprisoned, see?"

Bumble looked closer. She could see now that Nitsy and Pebblefoot were confined to some sort of cell. The Phantom was pacing, clawing at the walls. Nitsy appeared to be trying to reassure them both somehow.

"These are Drak times indeed if Phantom Pebblefoot finds himself at the mercy of He Who Shall No Longer Be CC'd," Penelope intoned.

Bumble stood, ready for action. "We must rescue Nitsy. Who knows what Drak has planned for them?" She turned to the computer, "How do I get to Drak's lair?"

Penelope motioned for Bumble to follow her. They took the elevator to the third floor. There, on aisle 78, row 4 Penelope pointed up at a container on the top shelf.

"Be a dear and fetch that down will you," she said.

"I can't reach," Bumble replied, "Is there a ladder?"

"No ladder."

"Then how...?" Bumble began.

"Have a little faith in yourself," said Penelope.

"But it's twelve feet up!"

"You asked how to help your friend. The answer is up on that shelf, but you'll have to reach for it Bumblerumpskin."

"Me? But I can't," Bumble whimpered.

"Bumble," declared Penelope in the voice of a school mistress. Bumble slumped against the racking. What did this blasted ghost want from her? Did she not understand?

"It's bigger than me, Penelope. Sometimes I get so overwhelmed by it all. I don't feel like a great Detector. Sometimes I feel like people know that I'm just a fraud and they're all running rings around me. I'm only as big as I am, so I'm sorry if that's not good enough." She crossed her arms to make her point.

Penelope straightened, as stern as a warning sign. "The world is a scary place Bumble, even for Detectors, that much is true. But you must have confidence in your abilities. Hang whatever people may be thinking; you must embrace your better qualities and fight for what you believe in!"

"That's a bit heavy, love," Bumble said, a little perturbed. "We only met this evening."

"Neither you nor your colleague have time for fairy airiness. Now reach over and grab that container like I told you!" Penelope was quite pink in her see-through face.

"Reach over?" Bumble turned and was surprised to see the once distant container right there in front of her. She looked down and gasped.

"Goshness," Bumble breathed. She was floating eight feet off the ground. Penelope was floating next to her, wearing an 'I told you so' face.

"I can fly?" Bumble confirmed.

"You're much more than a Detector, Bumble. That is only the beginning of your powers."

Dumbfounded, Bumble took the container from the shelf. It was empty.

"There's nothing in here," she said.

"Yes," replied Penelope, drifting back groundwards. Bumble followed, and landed a little wobbly, next to her. Penelope took the container and unfastened the lid.

"The quickest way to your colleague is the same route that Drak would have taken," she said. The lid popped off, then fell back into the jar. It disappeared. "Through Nothing."

Bumble watched as she upturned the container and poured its contents onto the floor. That's what it looked like, but Bumble couldn't see that anything had come out of the container.

"There's nothing there," said Bumble.

"Yes."

"Oh," Bumble said, getting it.

Penelope nodded. "Now in order to punch through All into Nothing, you will need to be travelling at quite some speed. That is assuming you know where you're going?"

Bumble smiled. She tied back her hair and fastened her shoelaces double-tight. Her face was a granite solid expression of determination. "Pebblefoot only comes out on moonlit nights. Whether he's a prisoner or not, what does that tell us about where Drak's lair might be?"

"You can't travel to the moon, dear," said Penelope, rather going against the grain of her previous can-do attitude.

"No. Drak had his lair built in the moon's reflection. That's where I'll find Nitsy."

With that Bumble lifted off from the ground and headed up to the ceiling. She poised herself above the puddle of nothing. It really did look like a solid floor. She looked down at her idol.

"Thank you Penelope. I won't forget your help. Good luck with the sale."

"You're welcome dear."

"If I succeed I'll come back and help you tidy up."

"Tidy up what, dear?"

"Call me Bumble."

"What?"

"Say Bumble."

"Bumble," Penelope obliged.

Bumble took a deep breath. "Bumble's my detectoring name. I'm on a mission now. Call me... Enigma Bitch."

The name sat sour on Penelope's tongue, but she got no chance to voice her distaste. In a pico second Bumble went from hovering quietly to hurtling towards the ground. Arms outstretched she burned through the air, headed straight for Nothing. Transonic waves rippled over her body as she broke the sound barrier. In an instant one thousand and thirty-seven containers shattered in the sonic boom. Bumble screamed as she hit the floor. Penelope Loveslice gawped as the newly minted Enigma Bitch disappeared at the speed of sound into the floor of the Negative department on the third floor of the Erstwhile & Somewhen Farmacopeoia.

Then she grabbed a broom and started to clean up after the ruddy girl.

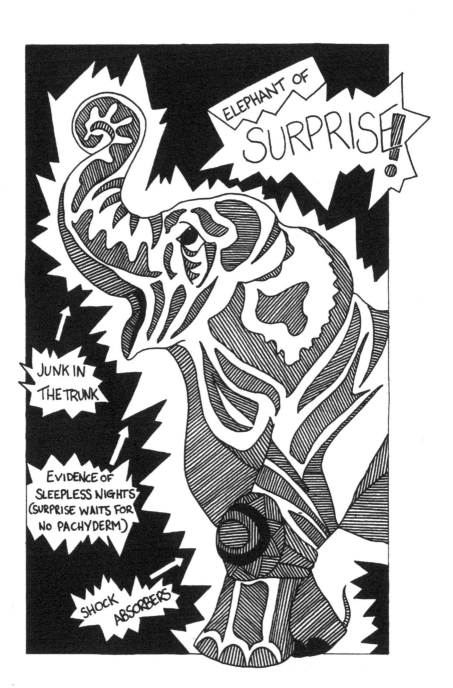

10

THE ELEPHANT OF SURPRISE

The moustache has ever been Mother Nature's moral barometer. That Adolf's moustache was tiny and he was bad, whereas Poirot's was quite big and he was a nice policeman. But then again there was Chaplin and Stalin and they threw the whole idea out of balance. Stupid. That whole theory amounted to nothing. A Nice crunchy bowl of Kellman's Schtopfelpops though, that would cheer everyone up. What were they? Small, wheat houses; like Monopoly houses but edible. Tiny houses with their tiny walls closing in ever tighter around their occupants. Move the walls. I can make walls; it used to be my job. And weeny wheat walls are no job at all, it's like pushing a Shreddie. It takes no effort at all to push a Shreddie, none at all. None. Nothing. Noth-

"Stop taking my air!" the Phantom howled. He launched himself onto Nitsy's back and clamped his hand over his mouth. Nitsy's detectorings failed in the madness and the cell walls seemed to leap a step closer, propelled by an invisible tide of Nothing, which to his tired mind had the sound of a stampede. Nitsy could only blink his suffocation, still paralysed by the Sabbath was he.

"The room's too small for both of us!" the Phantom ranted. "It's only right that you should give your life that I might live and trouble people's feet once again!"

The insanity gripped Nitsy within as the Phantom gripped him without. He focused his mind and fought against it. He detectored a Shreddie race; a gift set much like a Scalextrix given to a child at Christmas. In his mind he pushed his wheaty race car round the figure of eight, against the rumble of the living room crowd. In the sofa cushions they shouted so loud, a stampede of speed cereal fans, stomping and stomping. From nowhere the race track fell under a sweeping shadow. Christmas knitted finger square racing overcome by an avalanche of pebbles, swamping Nitsy with the pain of a stabby hurtfoot. He snapped back to reality.

"I can Project a thousand pebbles into your mind, Nitson! A million!" the Phantom hissed.

"Bumble," Nitsy muffled weakly.

"Yes, your little friend. As soon as she gets here I'll do for her too," said the Phantom.

The eyes in Nitsy's little purple face bulged, and not just because of the asphyxiation.

"Oh. You really believed that you and I were working for the same cause?"

Nitsy closed his eyes. How could he have been so stupid? He wasn't the Phantom's cellmate; he was the bait in a Bumbly trap.

"Of course I would never betray Drak, he's my mentor. That kind of loyalty can never be broken," the Phantom breathed into Nitsy's ear. "Not like your pathetic detectoring partnership. I knew all it would take to conquer you both was to divide you. I just exploited your silly bus stop barney. Neither of you has the courage of your beliefs."

With a horrendous laugh the Phantom tore the hats off Nitsy's head and drew him underarm in a final deathgrip. Nitsy felt what he knew was the last breath he'd ever take slip out of his body. His knees softened like warm camembert and he felt himself slide to the ground. The last thing he heard was the sound of Nothing, a stampede of doom that swallowed the room. It sounded like the charge of an elephant.

"Surprise!" Bumble yelled as she broke through the ceiling of the cell. She flew straight at the Phantom, knocking him to the floor in a thick candyfloss of plaster and sudden change. The three of them were thrown to the floor, dazed.

It was Nitsy who came to first. He sucked in the dust and blinked grit, as though his eyes were cement mixers. He could see that the cell was the same as it had always been. Its shrinking had been a Projection after all. He swam through the chaos to find Bumble. She was draped unconscious, but daintily, across a pile of rubble. He tried to revive her, but she was worryingly deep in snoozeland, her right eyebrow decorated with a stylish cut.

"Bumble!" Nitsy wailed. Behind him there was a scuff. The Phantom was back on his feet and bearing down on the battered Detectors. Nitsy stood up, blocking the path to Bumble. The Phantom simply pushed him over, and he tumbled down into the rubble with his lifeless partner.

The Phantom addressed the heavens, "I have them, Drak. As I promised."

There was silence. And then Philbert Drak spoke.

"Good. The great Detectors are now in my possession. Only one more thing is needed to complete my plan."

"Killing them, right?" said the Phantom.

"Well, two more things then."

Nitsy hugged Bumble close. He looked up at the hole in the ceiling that she had made. If he could somehow jump eight feet up into the air, reach down and haul up Bumble and do it all without Pebblefoot or the seemingly omnipresent Drak noticing, then they might have a chance at escape. Oh, who was he kidding? They were as dead as Penelope Loveslice or Darius Candlewick. Someone coughed.

"You're squishing my head," announced a small voice. It was Bumble. Nitsy looked down at her in his arms and loosened the vice-like grip he had on her brain.

"Thanks," she said.

"Two more things? The Phantom asked. "I was led to believe that killing these two daft Detectors would complete your return from Nothing and subjugation of the Earth's populace. Am I mistaken?"

"There is one more matter to attend to, but you need not concern yourself with that, Pebblefoot," Drak commanded. "What?"

The Phantom looked quite put out. "Well, while you've been sitting in prison dishing out orders I've been running around up here doing your bidding. I thought that might entitle me to be in on the whole plan."

"Now Phantom, don't have one of your moments."

The Phantom scowled.

"Bumble, can you move?" Nitsy whispered, "we have to get out of here. They're going to death us."

"Call me Enigma Bitch."

"Why?"

"I'm on a mish-huh-huh-hun..." Bumble spluttered. She had a coughing fit and lay back down. She was in no state to move. Nitsy knew it was up to him. He looked around for an alternative exit. The door to the cell was still locked, with nothing but a hand's width beneath it. There had to be another way. Then an idea arrived. It was Nity's best detectoring since he invented the Slightly Curved Washing Machine for Hotpoint. He rummaged in his knapsack and pulled out his long-gestating knitwear project; his 23 feet long stripy jumper.

"Bumble, we need to put this on."

Blearily, Bumble stared at the ridiculously long jumper. "You know I can't wear horizontal stripes, Nitsy."

"You have to trust me. Now you're going to put this on and then you're going to get on my shoulders, ok?"

Bumble nodded. She clambered into the jumper.

"Dammit Pebblefoot, I discovered you!" Drak boomed. "If you want any part of my future plans you will stop asking questions and do what I say. Kill them!"

The Phantom stomped his foot and spun round to leap on his quarry. He saw Bumble wearing a massive jumper hiked up around her waist, trying to climb onto Nitsy's back.

"Where do you think you're going?" he said and lunged at them. Bumble hoisted herself up. Now on Nitsy's shoulders she let the excess jumper fall to the floor. Stacked as they were they looked like an oversized stocking with a Bumble head.

"Now what?" she cried. "You know stripes make me look short."

"That's what I'm counting on!" said Nitsy.

The Phantom loomed over them just as the accumulated shortening effect of the stripes enveloping the Detectors took affect. They were reduced to the size of an insect. The Phantom recoiled in shock.

"I said KILL THEM!" Drak ordered.

The Phantom spotted the pea-sized micro-striped Detectors on the floor. He raised his foot above them.

"Detector this!" he spat with relish.

Teeny tiny Nitsy struggled to keep Bumble on his shoulders. "Fly, Bumble. Fly for the door!"

With all her might Bumble summoned forth the powers of Enigma Bitch. She held on tightly to Nitsy.

"Here we go!"

They lifted off, grazing the heel of Phantom Pebblefoot's boot as it drove into the rubble beneath them. Bumble struggled to keep them on course for the gap beneath the door.

"Nooooooo!" the Phantom yowled. Bumble and Nitsy flew under the door and out of the cell.

* * *

Bumble brought them to a landing when she was sure they were a safe distance from the holding cell and the clearly enraged Phantom. She climbed off Nitsy's shoulders and in throwing off the jumper they both returned to normal size.

"I knew you'd find me," said Nitsy. His voice was a bit wobbly. He turned away so Bumble couldn't see that his eyeballs were leaking. She handed him something. His peanut hat.

"Thought you were going to forget this," she said, gently.

He dried his eyes and blew his nose on the soft, machine washable peanut. Bumble put her own hat back on her head. "Thank you for holding onto it for me."

Then Bumble and Nitsy, Enigma Bitch and Clement Weatherfront, squirrel and peanut, whoever they were, they just hugged each other.

"Aw, innit cute," came Drak's voice. The Detectors turned to see Phantom Pebblefoot poised in front of them. He looked different though, angrier, and he spoke with Philbert Drak's voice. He rolled his shoulders as if trying on a new tank top.

"If you want something doing, do it yourself," he said.

"Is that you, Drak?" demanded Nitsy.

"Something I've learned in Nothing", he grinned, "the ability to take over people's minds. Luckily in this case it was practically empty anyway."

He crept closer to them. Bumble and Nitsy tried to shuffle away, but the ground wobbled beneath them. It was like they were standing on a waterbed.

"I had to start small of course," Drak continued, "Like as a mouse. I still managed to cause havoc that day though, I tell you."

Bumble's eyes narrowed. Phantom Drak sneered. "But you know that, don't you? How is Penelope these days? Still dead?"

Bumble shook with fury. How she wanted to wipe the smile off that face. She tightened her hat, the squirrel becoming a fearsome war mask.

"Did you know Drak, in some parts of the United States hazelnuts are known as Philberts? Well in a game of *Squirrel, Philbert, Phantom,* squirrel beats Philbert!" Bumble flew at Phantom Drak and nutted him in the face. He cowered, clutching his bloodied nose. Unable to do anything else he took off his boot and threw it at Bumble. It missed by a country parsec.

"Nits, the jumper!"

Nitsy grabbed the jumper and threw it over their nemesis. In a second Phantom Drak shrank to the size of a housefly. Bumble picked him up.

"Hey!" the little Phantom squeaked. "You can't do this to me! Forget you two! And forget you too, Drak! I never wanted to be part of your lame plan anyway!"

"Looks like the Phantom's mind is a size too small for Drak right now," Bumble observed. She took the Phantom's boot and squeezed the Phantom out of Nitsy's jumper. He plopped out like a blob from a miniature toothpaste tube and landed in the heel of his own boot. There he began to return to his own size.

"No!" he yelled. "Nooooooooooooooooo!"

"Caught, like a pebble in his own shrinking boot," said Nitsy.

"Only this time it's no Projection," said Bumble. The ground wobbled again. The ground that was grey dust, pocked with bunkers.

"Where are we?" Nitsy puzzled.

"The reflection of the moon," said Bumble, gathering up the now normal sized jumper. She looked up, where the night sky rippled as though it was painted on water. "Judging by the position of the stars I should say we're floating in Lake Windermere."

She jumped on Nitsy's shoulders and donned the jumper.

"We're going home, right?" said Nitsy.

"Oh, yes," Bumble confirmed, "It'll be easier to pass through the Barrier of Reflection if we're smaller though."

The jumper fell around Nitsy, again giving the illusion of one very tall Detector. That only lasted a moment or two, as they shrunk down to insect size once more. Bumble and Nitsy held onto each other as Bumble lifted them both off the ground. To anyone watching, it would seem that a tiny stripy bug was flying into a liquid moon.

"I'm a beeeeeeeeeeeeeeeeeeeeeeeeeeeeeeee!" Bumble sang.

"Weeeeeeeeeeeeeeeeeeeeeeeeeeeeeeeeeeeee!" Nitsy joined in.

11

AFTERTHOUGHTS

The first thing Bumble and Nitsy did was to go home and have crumble. Actually, if you want to be particular (and why shouldn't we be), first they returned to their normal size, put their Detector hats in the wash, attended to Bumble's cut. Then as Nitsy cued up the latest episode of *Whoops! Dinosaur Poo!* on the Pineapple TV box, Bumble telephoned the police.

She informed the Police Chief that Philbert Drak was gathering power and he now had the ability to strike out from his prison of

Nothing by taking other forms. That Phantom Pebblefoot had been working in league with Drak to capture not the Thinking Man's Trumpet, but the trumpet case, which, along with several thousand brass fasteners, would allow Drak to arm his Nothing army with the power to Project into the unsuspecting minds of the public. And also that Phantom Pebblefoot was responsible for the death of Professor Darius Candlewick, that Drak, while in mouse form, deathed Penelope Loveslice and that the former could be apprehended in the reflection of the moon on the surface of Lake Windermere, where he was trapped inside his own boot. Bumble paused to see if there was anything she had left out. She decided that was probably enough for the Police Chief to be going on with.

"Did you get all of that?" she asked. She realised she was speaking to a dial tone. "Hello?"

She hung up and flopped onto the sofa next to Nitsy.

"Look," Nitsy said, waving his arms about.

"What?"

"What day is it?" he asked, still waving and occasionally kicking his legs.

"Sunday," said Bumble.

"Exactly! I'm free!" Nitsy did a mini sofa dance. Bumble smiled, but she was troubled.

"When will they take us seriously, Nitsy?" she sighed.

Nitsy shook his head. "At least we take each other seriously," he said. Bumble nestled into the cushions.

"You know this isn't over don't you?"

"Drak said he only has one more thing to do before his plan is complete," Nitsy agreed.

"I've been thinking about that," Bumble yawned. "If Drak raises an army from Nothing then it will do him no good to arm them with Projecting trumpets."

"Because they have no thoughts to Project," said Nitsy. "Being from Nothing they are completely hollow, like Halloween pumpkins."

"Drak would somehow need to load all of the trumpets with some kind of thought or something". Bumble snuggled into the sofa.

"If only we knew where he would strike next," Nitsy murmured. Bumble didn't reply, because she was already asleep. Moments later Nitsy followed her into snoozeland. It had been a very long day for the Detectors.

* * *

Penelope Loveslice offered the teapot. The gentleman across the table waved his hand and declined another cup.

"I'd best be getting on," he said.

Penelope led him from the break room to the entrance of the Erstwhile & Somewhen Farmacopeoia. She held the door open for him.

"Thank you for stopping by, it was nice to meet you," she said.

"Likewise," the gentleman replied.

"It's so comforting to know that my business is going to be in safe hands. I must say, you have excellent farmacist credentials. You possibly know more about the applied use of daydreams than I do," Penelope paused. "You know, I'm surprised I've not heard your name before."

The gentleman grinned. He had the curious tick of shrugging his shoulders, as though he were trying on a new tank top. He slipped past her and outside.

"I shall email my agent and give him the go ahead on our deal," said Penelope moving things along. "Would, you like me to send you a copy?"

He called back, "just CC me in." Then he disappeared into the mist.

"Will do," Penelope said. She wasn't sure, but she swore she could detector something a little strange about the man. She decided it was nothing and went back into the Farmacopeoia for one last walk around her thoughts.

Especially that one persistent thought that she'd somehow left the iron on.

The End.

CASE NOTES

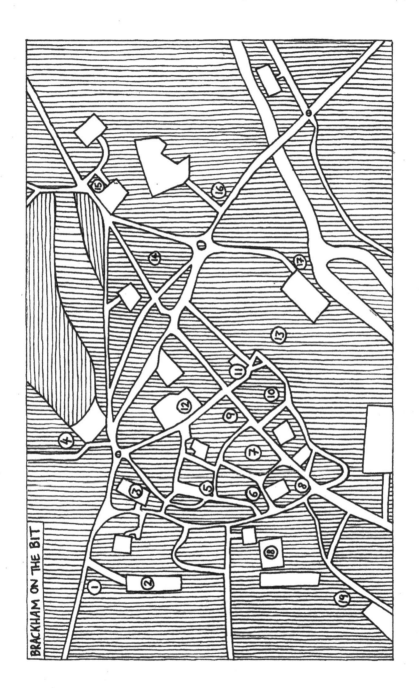

BRACKHAM ON THE BIT

1. *Farmacopeoia Lane*
2. *Particle Accelerator*
3. *Barry's Tinsel*
4. *Peacock Hatchery*
5. *Much Ado About Muffins*
6. *Pret a Nugget*
7. *Forest Millinery*
8. *Mauve Light District*
9. *BOTB Police Department*
10. *Bus depot*

11. *We Have Stationery*
12. *Brackham-on-the-Bit Daily Tribune*
13. *Vulgaris Common*
14. *Municipal Hell Portal*
15. *Channel 62 Studios*
16. *Walls Old Fashioned Walls*
17. *Natural Mystery Museum*
18. *Thought Kitchen*
19. *Sainsburg's Local*

PERSONS OF INTEREST

MOUSE

Mouse was a good 'un until he came a cropper at the pointy end of some devious Projection. Now he's a bit of a skilamalink, swift with the daddles and often ahead of the mutton-shunters. You could have been on his tail the whole time and not even have noticed.

PMAC

Paul is a creative loving spirit who writes, directs and makes things. He lives in Brighton. More about the things he makes can be found at **paulmacauley.net**

PMU

Phoebe is an artist and illustrator from Hove Actually. More of her stuff can be found **pmuink.com** where she posts daily doodles to foster positive drawing habits.

3AM ON A FRIDAY IN JANUARY

Captain America is on my bum when I get the call. It's the dark middle of a winter's night and I'm dressed only in my Marvel superhero pants when I'm woken from my sleep by my phone, Ivan Pomme VI. It's my creative partner, PMu, waffling like some deranged breakfast appliance. Sensing her urgency, and fearing that this will again turn out to be the wonky end of another 3 day inking bender, I hustle myself and the Avengers out of bed, careful not to wake the inhabitants of the Lego town on my bedroom floor. In the kitchen of my basement loft apartment I put on some coffee. Then, feeling the chill, I opt instead for a shirt and trousers.

I ask PMu to begin again. The details she shares sound unlikely, ill-conceived and slightly annoying. I'm intrigued. The gist: PMu's PA Eggward Wulfmausen had taken a call from a Nonny Mouse asking for a meeting with us about a story which might be of interest. Eggward had taken down the details, capturing as well as a Chihuahua can the details of a suggested rendezvous. Having deciphered his paw writing, PMu asks if we will answer the call to adventure? I think about going back to bed. Then she mentions the word 'Detectors'. Barely a moment is existed before we are en route to the bins behind Aldi on the London Road.

Scanning moonlit Biffas for our nameless contact, PMu is trepidatious but I am downright fearful of a trap, and can take only small comfort from the bolstering presence of Iron Man on my left buttock. From the blackness comes a small but demanding voice. I am startled and instinctively I go on the offensive, launching a powerful attack into the shadows. The counter attack is swift and, struck directly in Thor, I go to the floor. The voice introduces itself as one Nitson von Nitzenjammer. The name rings a bell like a cricket ball striking Big Ben (in actual fact Big Ben is the name of the person who cleans the clock, not the bell itself). I'd heard of the Detectoring duo known as Bumble and Nitsy, but had written off the possibility that they might exist as so much whimsy. Yet here, stepping into the dim light, is one of them. And he has a story to tell.

It is not often one gets to meet a Detectoring celebrity, even rarer is it that one gets the chance to capture one of their adventures. I have always admired those who sense deeply both into the world and into their imagination, and who recognise that both are as real and essential as the other. As Nitsy tells his tale me and PMu chase truths like butterflies, capturing them in our form-nets and nailing them to reality until this simile stops working. PMu is sketching with her portable apparatus (pencil) and I scribble on any surface I can find, our creative flow stronger than a waterfall in a shampoo advert. The sun is coming up like the night just popped some pills and we are still writing, still drawing when finally Nitsy comes to his story's end.

We are exhausted. Nitsy takes his leave. PMu and me have so many questions, chief among them "what are we meant to do with all this?"

Nitsy pauses and says simply "Tell the people what happened". And like that he is gone, just another person waiting 17 minutes for a bus. PMu and I look at our surroundings, which are rendered somehow less glamorous in the seagull soundtracked morning light. But on every bin, every wall, every inch of tarmac are our words and pictures, pieces of a story that has to be told. It is beautiful and confusing and I feel alive and sick.

We head for Ritabix Mansions to try to make sense of it all. We are a whirl of details, feelings, chances and happenings. Something about a trumpet, a mouse, a few villains and exotic place names like Brackham-on-the-Bit. I have no idea where to start and feel under qualified and out of my depth -it's like we're trying to make a cake from detonated ingredients using only chopsticks. Then quietly, calmly, PMu orders the pizza and we begin our work to bring Bumble and Nitsy's story to life. PMu and PMac bossing it like the Avengers. No, better than that. Like Detectors.

APPRECIATIONS

The publication of this book happened with the support of a group who wanted to read it and so backed our crowdfunding campaign to bring it into existence. These brilliant people will forever be part of the journey of this book. For putting up your hand and saying "yes, we'll come along with you!" our heartfelt gratitude goes out to Alison Roberts, Andy Foreman, Annie Sutton, Briony "Jaffa Cake" Jefferies, Carla Gilfoyle, Charlie Peverett, Charlotte Grosvenor, Chloe "Sully" Sullivan, Chris "Bloke" Macauley, Chris & Faye Bedford, Christine Garner,

Dad & Jane, Dan Hedley, Danny Leach, Diccon Spain, Didj & Finn, Dutch Frankel, Ellen Power, Emma "Emmo" Farrugia, Emmie Spencer, Gary O'Connell, Giorge Bainbridge, Holly Jennings, James Macauley, Jenny Warwick, Jo Spain, John & Denise, John & Gill Munson, Joseph Daly, Joss Sadler and Ethan Sadler, Katie Felton, Katie "The Untruth Fairy" Merrien, Laura Mousseau, Martina Silla, Matt Hinson, Max de la Nougerede, Michelle Eades, Natalie Stavrou, Natalie "Natterjacks" Blunt, Nick Quirke, Peta Rabson, Rhodri Alexander, Rita Garner, Sarah McKellen, Sergio Eduardo Martínez Solis, Sonia Babister, Susie Stavert, Tamsin Bishton, Tim Cook, Una Nicholson and Zoe "Sparkly Kittenlicks" Nicholson.

Before the book even found these supporters we were lucky to have the encouragement and feedback of a wonderful few who helped us to whip the thing into shape. T-Bish, thank you for being our friend when we needed to hear that what we were doing was worthwhile, and for giving us feedback and telling us to get on with it. Angie and Kerry, thank you for your generosity, your honest notes and your invaluable attention to detail, which gave us confidence to finally press 'print'.

And before there were any words or pictures to share there was a person without whom there would have been no cause to tell this story in the first place. Thank you Katy, a.k.a. the real Bumble.

Finally, thank you, reader. You chose to read this story over doing anything else in this cosmos of infinite possibility. Nice one. Now go and make things. Especially moments of wonder, of togetherness and of *fun*.

by Nitson von Nitzenjammer

The Case of the Rinky-Dink Happenings

The Case of the Unexpected Question?

The Case of the Case of The

Recipe for Disaster:
A young Detector's notes from The Thought Kitchen

The Crumble Sutra

Babies vs Peacocks: when will the fighting end?